TOMB STONE HAND

RICK VEITCH

Tombstone Hand
by Rick Veitch

A Panel Vision™ Book

Published by
SUN COMICS
PO BOX 1371
West Townshend, VT 05359
rarebit@sover.net
rickveitch.com

First Edition
February 2021

ISBN: 9798587306875

Thanks: Bo Diddley, Dashiell Hammett,
Charles Brownstein

for Sergio and Ennio

GILA BEND, ARIZONA

·

1926

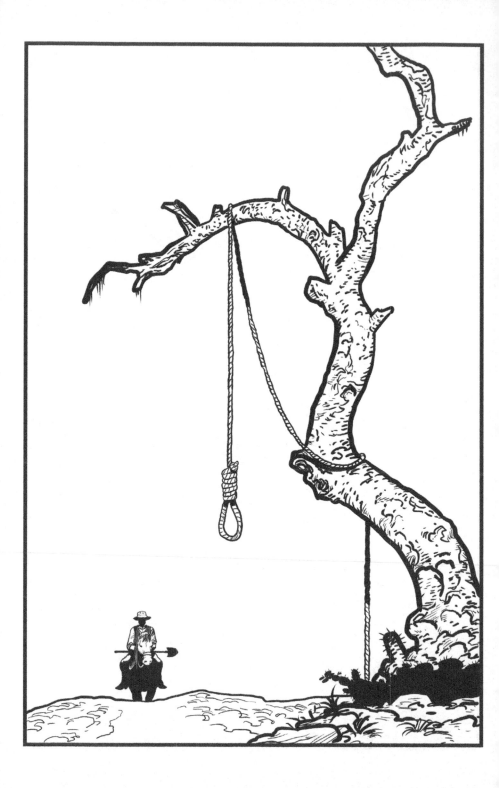

THAT MEANS YOUR TIME'S COMIN' SOONER RATHER THAN LATER.
TODAY'S YOUR LUCKY DAY, SLIVER.

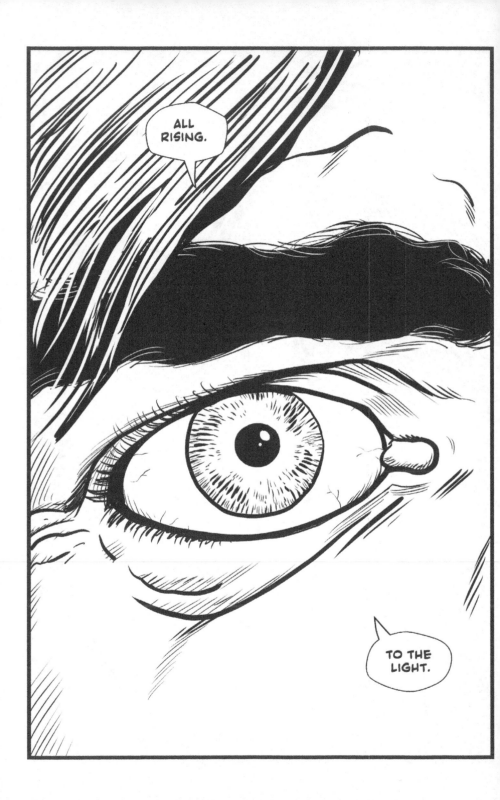

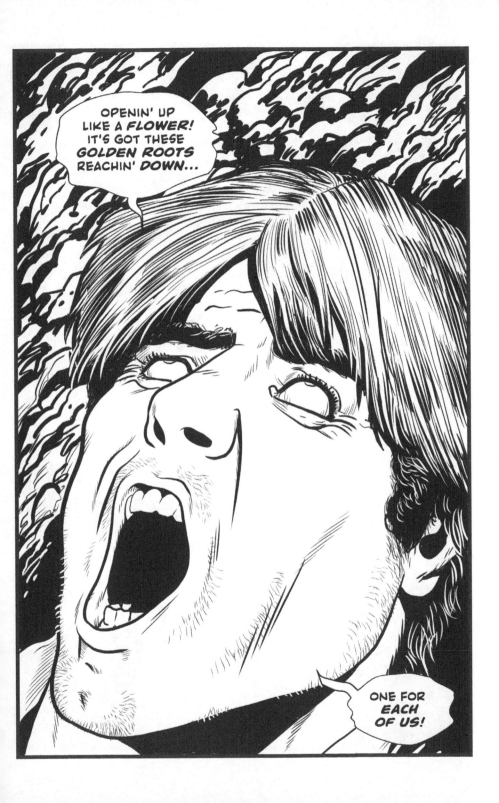

WHAT ARE THEY SAYIN'?
WHAT ARE THEY DOIN'?
DAMN YOUR EYES, SLIVER-- Y'CAN'T DIE AND LEAVE ME HANGIN'!

SHALL IT BE THE COUP DE GRACE WITH MY MAUSER?
OR THE GALLOWS?
YOUR CHOICE.

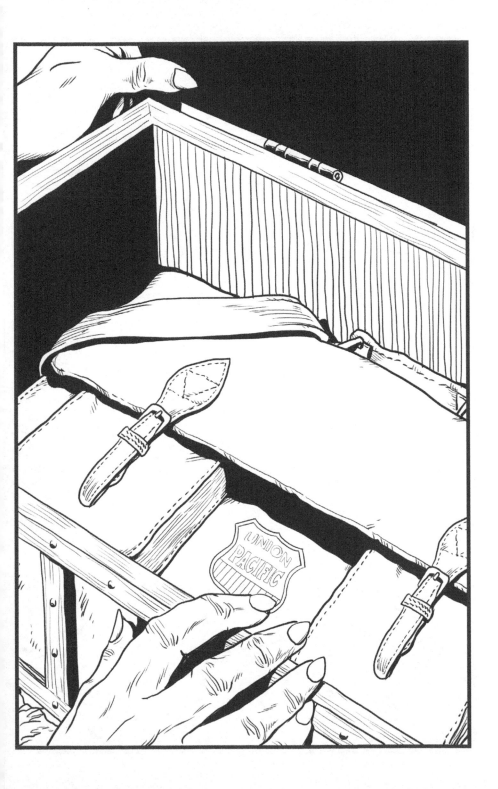

Other
PANEL VISION™
titles:

Super Catchy

The Spotted Stone

Otzi

Redemption

Graphic Novels by Rick Veitch

The Maximortal

Brat Pack

The One

Abraxas and the Earthman

Army@Love

Can't Get No

Heartburst

Shiny Beasts

Greyshirt: Indigo Sunset

Rabid Eye

Pocket Universe

Crypto Zoo